Glow in the Dark
What's Under My Bed?

Written by Victoria Sherrow
Illustrated by Mary Grace Eubank

A GOLDEN BOOK • NEW YORK

Western Publishing Company, Inc., Racine, Wisconsin 53404

Jenny was buttoning her pajamas when suddenly there was a monster standing beside her bed!

"*Grrrrooooooarrrr!*" growled the monster. Its face was green and lumpy and its mouth was full of jagged teeth.

Then Jenny noticed that the monster was dressed like her brother, Rob. It wore a red-striped T-shirt and blue jeans and had a baseball cap sticking out of its pocket.

"Ugh!" said Jenny. "Why the creepy face?"

"It's part of my costume for the school play," said Rob as he took off the mask. "I scared you, didn't I?"

Jenny shook her head. "No, I knew it was you all the time."

"Ha!" Rob laughed.

"OK, you two," called their mother. "It's bedtime."

As Rob ran across the hall to his room, Jenny looked around and shivered. Sometimes she was afraid to be alone in her room at night. Strange sounds seemed to come from the walls. Weird shadows appeared near her bed.

"Well, at least I have Arabella," thought Jenny, tucking her favorite doll under the bedcovers. "And I have my night-light." She pulled the chain, but the light did not come on.

Jenny called out, "Mom, my night-light isn't working!"

Her mother came in and looked at the light. "I'm sorry, Jen," she said. "The bulb must have blown out. I'll get a new one tomorrow."

"But, Mom, I need my night-light tonight," said Jenny.

"Scaredy-cat, afraid of the dark," Rob hooted from the hall.

"Don't tease your sister, Rob," said their mother. "Now both of you go to sleep."

Jenny climbed into bed and pulled the covers up to her chin. That way, she would be safe when her mother turned out the light.

Under the covers, Jenny held Arabella tight and shut her eyes. She heard a small noise—*tap, TAP, tap, TAP*—coming from somewhere in the apartment.

Then came a strange creaking and rattling noise.
Creeeak—chuk, chuk, chuk, chuk—tap, TAP... went the noises.
Jenny pictured a ghost clumping through the apartment. Then she imagined a monster—an ugly monster with a face like Rob's mask...

Jenny opened her eyes. Light from car headlights shone in from the street and made scary shadows on her walls.

The stuffed animals on Jenny's shelf looked strange in the moving lights. They seemed to stare at Jenny. And her collection of play-dress-up hats seemed to grow faces!

I'll *never* fall asleep, thought Jenny. Should she cover the hats with a blanket? No, that would mean crossing the floor barefoot in the dark. Then Jenny remembered that she had not looked under her bed before her mother left the room! Every night, she checked her closet and the dark empty space under the bed before going to sleep.

The room seemed creepier than ever. Jenny heard more tapping and creaking, rattling sounds. She covered her head with the pillow.

Suddenly she heard a loud *BANG!*

Jenny sat straight up in bed and Arabella slid to the floor.
Jenny leaned down to get her doll and saw a horrible monster
under her bed!

"Mommy!"

Her mother ran into the room. "Jenny, what's wrong?"

"A m-m-monster," Jenny said. "Under my b-b-bed."

Her mother reached down. "Here's your monster," she said, holding up a rubbery mask.

Jenny peeked out from the covers. Ugh—it was Rob's creepy monster mask.

Her mother frowned. "I'll have to ask your brother how this got here."

But Rob was already standing in Jenny's doorway. "I'm sorry, Jenny," he said. "I didn't think it would scare you so much."

"It didn't," said Jenny, "but I heard lots of creepy noises—tapping, rattling, and a creaking sound."

"Me too," said Rob. "I heard a loud bang."

Their mother looked puzzled, then she smiled. "Come with me. I think I know where the noises came from."

They walked into the living room. The sewing machine was on a table, and new striped curtains hung at the windows. "The loud noise you heard was me dropping the hammer when I put up our new curtains," said their mother.

"What about the tapping?" asked Jenny.

Their mother thought for a minute, then she pushed the rocking chair back and forth. "Does that sound like the tapping noise?"

Jenny nodded.

"I had to move this to reach the windows," their mother said. "It probably rocked for a minute. And this old sewing machine of mine sure does rattle and creak!"

"I guess there's nothing to worry about," said Jenny. "But I do wish I had my night-light."

"I can fix that," Rob said. He went into his room and came back with his old night-light. "I bet it still works." He plugged the light in near Jenny's bed and turned it on.

Jenny grabbed Arabella and got under the covers. Her room seemed cozy and friendly again. Especially now that no monsters were under the bed!